THE RENEGADE

A PREQUEL TO THE HARD EDGE OF MAGIC

THE RUPTURED KINGDOM
BOOK 1.5

ALLAN N. PACKER

LUMINANT PUBLICATIONS

THE RUPTURED KINGDOM SERIES

The Hard Edge of Magic (Book 1)
The Riven Land (Book 2)
…other titles to come

Companion Novelette
The Renegade: A Prequel to The Hard Edge of Magic

Other epic fantasy by Allan N. Packer

THE STONE CYCLE SERIES

The Stone of Knowing (Book 1)
The Cost of Knowing (Book 2)
The Stone of Authority (Book 3)
The Struggle for Authority (Book 4)
The Stone of Vitality (Book 5)
The Hope of Vitality (Book 6)

Companion Novelettes
The Seer: A Prequel to The Stone of Knowing
The Rending: A Prequel to The Cost of Knowing

The Renegade
A Prequel to The Hard Edge of Magic

The Ruptured Kingdom (Book 1.5)

Copyright © 2024 by Allan N. Packer

First edition (v1.0) published in 2024
by Luminant Publications

ISBN 978-1-925898-87-3

Luminant Publications
PO Box 305
Greenacres, South Australia 5086

http://www.allanpacker.com

Cover Design by 100 Covers

Map illustration by Brian Plush

THE RENEGADE
A PREQUEL TO THE HARD EDGE OF MAGIC

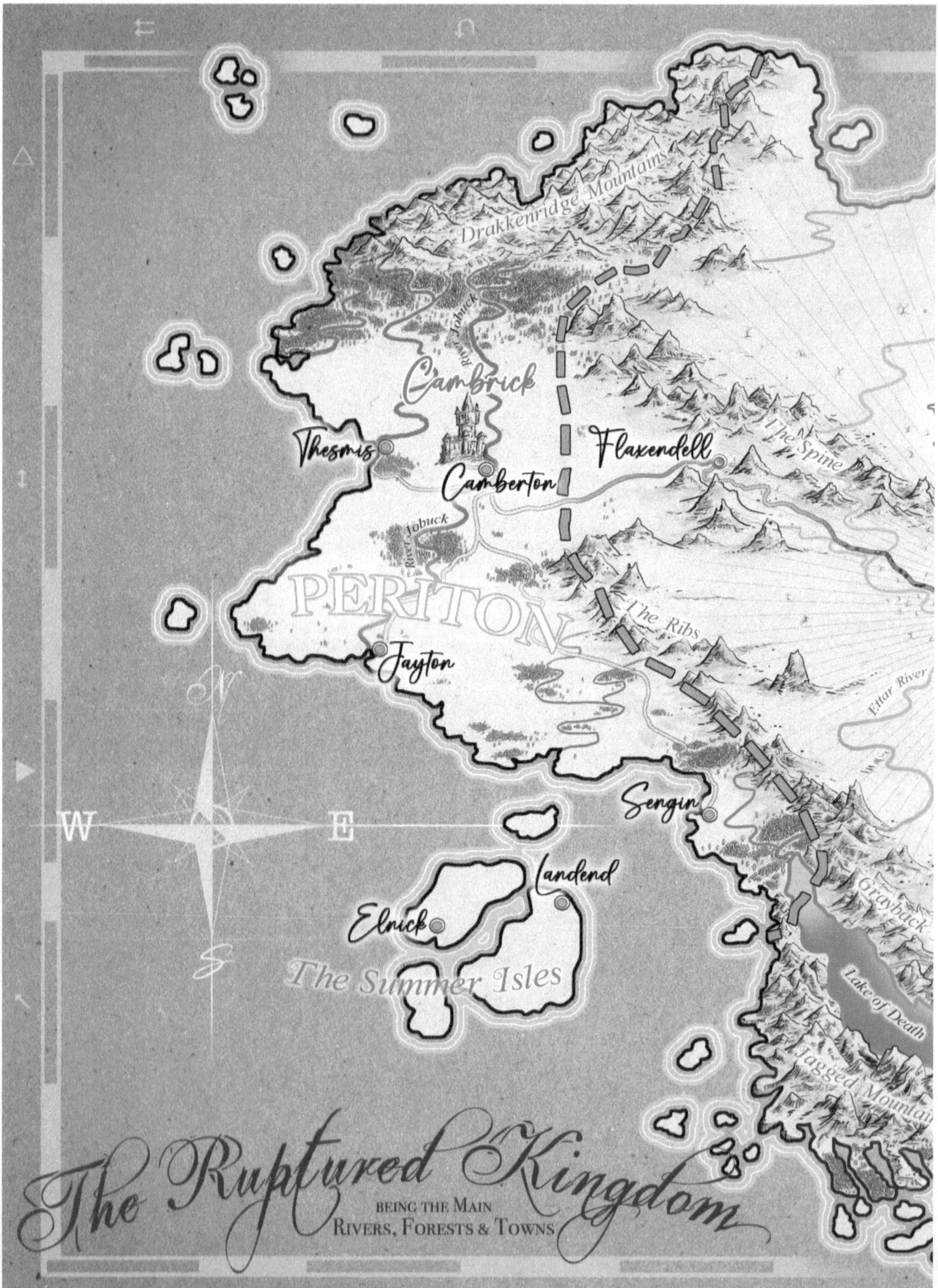

Drakkenridge Mountains
River Jobuck
Cambrick
Thesmis
Camberton
Flaxendell
The Spine
River Jobuck
PERITON
The Ribs
Jayton
Eltar River
Sengin
Landend
Grayback
Elnick
The Summer Isles
Lake of Death
Jagged Mountains
N
S
W
E
The Ruptured Kingdom
BEING THE MAIN
RIVERS, FORESTS & TOWNS

Northport
Forshem
METHESIA
Ruined Kingdom
Ettaran
Ettar River
Souther
Bane Mountains
Mountains
Brynford
Brynburn River
Firetip Mountains
TANTEL
Antilin
River Antil
Shelmar
Dynsdale
Nairb H Sulp • Royal Cartographer & Geographer • High Street • Cambrick

CHAPTER 1

Stooping low in the confined space, Dalthinir crept forward through the darkness, pursued by the faint echoes of his footsteps. With every step taking him further from fresh air and open skies, he derived what comfort he could from the flickering light of his torch.

Someone or something had carved this tunnel in the rock. Its walls were unnaturally smooth and its dimensions unvarying, vaguely like the neck of a giant bottle. It led unerringly downward at a steady angle.

The tunnel soon opened into a large natural cavern. Straightening his back in relief, he slowly stretched before peering around.

Near the tunnel entrance he spotted a small grotto. Reaching it in a few steps, he thrust his torch inside. To his astonishment he found a small table with a chair beside it. An oil lamp stood on the table, and after a moment's hesitation he bent to light it.

He glanced about curiously as the lamp's yellow glow flooded the grotto. Parchments were strewn across the table. His heart beat faster when a document titled *Rudiments of Dragon Magic* caught his eye. Then he noticed *Dark Magic—Myths and Realities*, bearing the name of the author, *Master Arbilis*. Dalthinir knew enough history to recognize that name. Master Arbilis had lived in Ettaran in the dying days of the kingdom of Methesia, before the Great Desolation.

He soon spotted more of the same. Plenty more.

Texts like these were strictly forbidden, and for good reason. Dabbling with dragon magic was perilous, and not just for the person involved. Power of this kind was unpredictable and uncontrollable, and it could be highly destructive. Every mage knew it.

Then he noticed a seal lying beside a lump of red wax. Picking it up, he examined it carefully. It featured a crouching dragon over a scroll. The scroll symbol identified its owner as a mage, and only one mage used a seal with a crouching dragon. Looking more closely he saw letters on the table addressed to the same person.

He had found Master Banadin's sanctuary. And the mage was actively engaged in prohibited research. It was worse than Dalthinir had imagined.

It remained only to exit the tunnel and return swiftly with senior members of the Compact—the council of mages—to show them the evidence. Chief Master Sentaris, the head mage, was too old and frail to enter the tunnel, but his deputy Master Adrastas would surely be willing to come.

A sudden echo set him on edge. Swiftly blowing out the oil lamp, he used a tiny burst of magic to extinguish his torch as well. Then he stepped cautiously out of the grotto, every sense alert.

Someone was coming down the tunnel. Could they have seen his light? He groped around the edge of the cavern, away from the tunnel and the grotto, desperate to find somewhere to hide. Colliding with an outthrust of rock in the dark, he scurried around it and hid himself on the far side.

His farsense had revealed nothing. That would normally have suggested whoever was heading his way was not a mage. But for some strange reason his farsense had been blocked since the moment he entered the tunnel. Some property in the rock must allow it to mask magical auras. No other conclusion made sense.

A tiny light grew slowly brighter. As its bearer emerged from the tunnel, Dalthinir's farsense was awakened. Every mage had a unique magical aura—also referred to as magical glimmer, or more often just glimmer—and from the new arrival's glimmer he saw at once that it was Banadin. He might frequent this place, but why did he have to appear at that particular moment? Dalthinir shook his head in frustration.

Peering around the rock he saw Banadin disappear into the grotto. He busied himself there for several minutes. Dalthinir considered sneaking past him to reach the tunnel, but he quickly decided it was too risky.

Banadin soon emerged. The light from his torch showed him carrying a bulging sack.

Dalthinir's heart sank. The mage had probably just removed anything of interest from the grotto.

Banadin's light bobbed toward the tunnel before stopping completely. Dalthinir could see him outlined in its mouth.

"Whoever you are, I know you're there!" he called. "I've had the mouth of the tunnel watched, and I was on my way here when you went in. My sentry recognized your robe, so I know you're a mage. I don't know why you came here snooping on me, but I trust you made the most of your brief opportunity to examine my documents and personal papers. You won't get a second chance, because I've just removed them all."

A harsh laugh sounded before he continued. "I've enjoyed this little haven, isolated as it is. Until you interfered, it was the perfect location to do my research without interruption. No matter. I'm ready to move on. I hope you enjoy the cavern as much as I did, because you won't be leaving it. Not ever!"

Having said it, he turned away and hurried up the tunnel.

Before Dalthinir could react in any way, a rumble sounded, growing in volume until it shook the cavern. A seemingly endless avalanche of rock poured down, completely burying the grotto and the tunnel entrance. Stepping away from the tunnel instinctively, he hastily surrounded himself with a magical shield to protect himself from falling rocks.

As soon as the rumbling ceased he removed his shield, only to be covered from head to toe with dust. The cavern was filled with it, and he could barely breathe. He hurriedly reinstated his shield, but the air inside his shield was barely breathable. He was reduced to coughing helplessly.

To his immense relief the air slowly cleared. Although he could breathe once more, it was too early for celebration. He was trapped underground with no way out.

Desperate as his situation might seem, he saw no real cause for alarm. Banadin had himself acknowledged he didn't know which mage he had trapped. That meant he couldn't know that his victim, like him, had the ability to move objects magically. Dalthinir saw no obvious reason why he couldn't dig himself out.

He began by using his elements ability with fire to create a magical fireball. With illumination available, he began removing boulders from the huge pile blocking the tunnel entrance.

The task proved much bigger than he had imagined. Banadin had undoubtedly used his own magical abilities to trigger the rockfall, but it was hard to imagine he could have anticipated the extent of his success. The amount of rock blocking the entrance was astonishing.

The trapped mage worked doggedly until he reached the point where he could barely continue. Just when he began to hope that the tunnel might be in reach, loud rumbles sounded once more.

Throwing a shield around himself was almost beyond him, but somehow he managed it, even as the rocks came pouring down. The second rockfall dwarfed the first. He had to wait many minutes before it was safe to remove his shield. Even then the dust had not entirely settled.

It was now clear that digging his way out was unrealistic. Even if he could find the energy to remove enough rock to reach the tunnel, there was no telling what new collapse he might provoke in the process.

For the first time it occurred to him that with the tunnel blocked, he would eventually run out of air. He fought down a wave of panic.

Air was far from his only problem. Apart from Banadin, no one knew where he was. If anyone searched for him, the rock that entombed him would apparently mask his glimmer. And even if others knew exactly where he was, how could they burrow through so much rock in time to reach him?

Perched on a rock in the darkness, Dalthinir tried to calm himself. Drawing upon his elements power he sent a fireball floating high into the air, using the illumination to peer intently around the cavern as it slowly drifted down. No obvious way of escaping presented itself.

The piece of wood he had used for a torch was still at hand, and he relit it with his magic. Pitiful as it seemed in the darkness, the glow of the torch offered him some comfort.

He passed a hand slowly over his face, trying to come to terms with his own folly. What had he been thinking? He should never have entered the tunnel without first informing someone else of what he was doing.

Banadin hadn't known which mage had discovered his sanctuary, because he didn't have Dalthinir's ability to detect glimmer using farsense. So even he didn't know the identity of the person he had trapped underground. He'd find out soon enough, of course—it would be whichever mage had mysteriously disappeared without trace.

He shook his head in dismay.

As he sat brooding, he allowed his mind to wander, recalling the events that had brought him to that place at that moment.

It had all begun with a conversation with Lord Platten, a nobleman known to Dalthinir through his parents.

"Do you have any idea what your fellow mages are up to?" the noble had asked gruffly.

He shook his head curiously.

"It's that Master Banadin fellow," the noble growled. "He tried to sign me up for some nefarious scheme he's hatching. Most irregular! I refused to have anything to do with it."

"What kind of scheme?"

"Something to do with using magic on a grand scale to overturn the established order. A lot of nonsense if you ask me. Dangerous nonsense!"

Dalthinir had frowned, uncertain what to make of it. "That's odd. I'm not sure what to say to you."

"Say what you like, boy," Lord Platten had said. "But make sure your people keep a close eye on him!"

Dalthinir suppressed a snort. He had attained the status of mage, entitling him to the honorific of Master, and he'd achieved it well before he reached his current age of thirty. He couldn't imagine any measure by which he could still be classed as a boy.

"I'll see what I can find out," he replied.

In spite of his promise he had given it little thought when he was spotted two days later by a city official he had known since childhood.

"Master Dalthinir! Did you hear about Lord Platten?" Seeing his blank look, the official had pressed on. "He's been murdered!"

"Murdered? Surely not! I spoke to him only recently."

"It's true. It happened on the afternoon of the day before last. A man has been charged with the murder. Apparently this man received an anonymous letter containing clear evidence that his wife had been involved in an affair some years previously." He nodded knowingly. "Not surprisingly, it raised questions about the paternity of his heir."

"How did this affect Lord Platten?"

"He was named as the other party in the affair. When the man confronted his wife, she didn't deny it. So he stormed over to Lord Platten's mansion in a rage. A violent argument followed. When it ended the nobleman was dead!"

Dalthinir was appalled. "That's terrible!"

"Terrible, yes, but a straightforward case at least. A simple crime of passion."

They parted with Dalthinir shaking his head. On the surface, the two incidents seemed entirely unrelated.

Nevertheless it occurred to Dalthinir to wonder who had sent the letter. Was it possible that Banadin had done it as a way of silencing a person who knew too much about his plans? That would have required him to have had a letter ready when he first approached Lord Platten. It seemed much too calculated to be plausible.

Nevertheless, Dalthinir decided to do what he had promised the late nobleman and keep an eye on Master Banadin.

His ability to detect magical auras would prove useful, since it allowed him to identify and track mages without needing to follow them. Each mage radiated a characteristic magical aura, or glimmer. While every mage could detect the use of magical power with farsense, only a very few mages, himself among them, were also able to detect magical glimmer. His own ability was strong, allowing him to detect glimmer from a considerable distance. He was easily able to cover the entire city.

Over the following days his farsense revealed that Banadin was spending significant time with a number of other mages, meeting them one at a time. Dalthinir was able to identify each of them from their glimmer. Three were experienced and well-established, while two others were more junior.

Banadin routinely left the city with one or other of them for an entire morning or afternoon. It might mean nothing, but it seemed unusual behavior.

He was also spending a lot of time alone within the city but away from his dwelling. He consistently headed toward the cliff at the rear of the city.

Dalthinir had no intention of eavesdropping on Banadin when he was with one of the other mages. He had no mandate for such a clear violation of their privacy. But he saw no reason not to find out where Banadin was going on his own. Farsense showed him where to look, but the specific location eluded him. Inexplicably, he was able to sense the mage only when he was in the open—his glimmer seemed to disappear when he reached the cliff face. The only logical conclusion was that he was entering a cave, although that should not have obscured his magical aura.

For several days Dalthinir searched fruitlessly along the cliff face, hunting for an entrance. Finally, at dusk the previous day, his farsense had alerted him to the presence of a mage. Peering through the half light from his vantage point in the shadow of a large house, he spotted a furtive figure slipping away from the cliffs to disappear into the bustle of the city. His farsense told him it was Banadin. He decided to return the next day to explore the location.

The city of Cambrick, capital of the kingdom of Periton, had been built at the base of a towering cliff. A massive protective wall stretched in a sweeping semicircle around the city, with the cliff anchoring the wall at each end. The rocks that formed the cliff were smooth, but rarely completely vertical. They were also hard and difficult to work. Occasionally used to provide the back wall of a dwelling, they were mostly shunned by builders.

Arriving soon after dawn, Dalthinir had approached the cliff, searching for an opening. Coming upon the tumbledown ruins of a small dwelling, he had almost passed it by. Then on impulse he entered the remains of the building, picking his way over the rubble that littered the floor.

Unusually, the building had been built against the cliff face. Making his way to the native rock, at first he saw nothing unusual. Then he felt a slight movement of cold air. There must be an opening somewhere. In one corner of the room a large piece of matting hung limply over what had once been a wall. Carefully pushing it aside, he found a dark opening. A tunnel, not quite tall enough to stand up in, led downward into the mountain.

Picking up a length of broken wood from the floor, he used his elements ability with fire to light the end of it. Holding up his torch, he stepped into the tunnel. As soon as he released the hanging, it fell back over the opening, leaving him in total darkness with only his torch to provide a glimmer of light. A few minutes later he had arrived in the cavern.

Now, thanks to Banadin, he was stranded there.

As the hours passed, he explored the edges of the cavern. Finding a trickle of water in one corner, he used it to slake his thirst. Beyond that, there was nothing to offer any kind of encouragement.

It was impossible to guess the time, but eventually he began to feel weary. Lying down on the rocky floor, he tried to calm himself for sleep.

He soon discovered he was incapable of resting. How could he relax when he knew no help was coming? If he couldn't find a way to save himself, he would die there alone.

CHAPTER 2

Time had lost all meaning for Dalthinir. He had no way of telling if it was day or night under the open sky. Perhaps two days and two nights had passed since he entered the cavern. Certainly he had fallen asleep twice, although it had been extremely fitful on both occasions.

Before his piece of wood burned to nothing he had explored the cavern as best he could. He found nothing to suggest there was any other way out. His initial concerns about running out of air did at least seem unfounded. Fresh air was somehow finding a way into the enclosed space. Perhaps a vent was concealed in the high ceiling of the cavern.

He had plenty of fresh water to drink, but hunger had become a constant companion. The likely outcome was that he would die of starvation. He refused to dwell on it.

He wondered who would miss him. In recent years he had lost both of his parents, and he had no siblings. He'd heard himself described as well-liked, but he could not imagine anyone being inconsolable over losing him.

His thoughts turned to Inga, as they often had of late. The two of them were similar in age, and she had joined the Compact no more than twelve months after him. He had noticed her immediately. Unfailingly kind and gentle, she was soon seen by her fellow mages as a reliable shoulder to cry on.

After he finally admitted to himself that he was drawn to her, it was only his natural shyness that prevented him from actively pursuing her. It was long past time for him to declare his interest, and of late he had been summoning his courage to do just that.

She had powerful farsense ability, and like him she was able to detect magical auras. It had occurred to him to ask her to keep a check on his whereabouts when he began following Banadin. But he'd decided against it, concerned that she might regard his suspicions as ungenerous.

Even if she had been looking for him, it almost certainly wouldn't have helped. Magical glimmer was not normally blocked by anything except water, yet the rock that entombed him seemed different. He was unable to detect glimmer in the outside world, so she wouldn't be able to find him either.

Sitting alone in the dark, his regrets threatened to overwhelm him. Stretching out on the rock once more, he sought the sweet oblivion of slumber.

When sleep eventually took him, he dreamed.

He stood in the same cavern, although it was dimly illuminated, revealing every rock in every hidden corner. The source of the light was not visible. Looking up he saw a huge moth fluttering near the roof of the cavern. As he watched, it disappeared into a crack in the rock.

All at once he found himself floating rapidly upward in pursuit of the moth. The crack was too small to admit his body, but even so he followed it in. Strangely, he was in no way alarmed by what was happening.

The moth flittered back and forth, following a draft of air upward. Even surrounded by a mountain of rock, there was never a hint of darkness in the journey. The light was slowly growing brighter, and Dalthinir sensed that the source of the brightness lay above him.

Abruptly the narrow passage followed by the moth broadened into a vast cavern, many times the size of the one in which he was trapped.

Lying on the floor of the cavern lay a huge dragon. Resplendently sheathed in magic, and golden in color with streaks of blue on its wings, the dragon appeared to be sleeping.

Ignoring the gigantic creature, the moth fluttered ever higher, passing once more into a narrow passage in the roof of this latest cavern.

How long they traveled he couldn't tell, but eventually the light grew so bright it was blinding. Suddenly the moth shot out of the rock. Following, he found himself in the open, with the cliff top below him. The city of Cambrick lay far below. If he'd been gifted with wings, he could have glided down to land in the city streets.

Instead he abruptly found himself back in the cavern where he had started. This time he became aware of water rushing inside the rock. The noise of it filled his ears. Approaching the trickle of water where he had been slaking his thirst, he examined it closely. It was seeping through the rock from the nearby river.

Without warning he passed through the rock, finding himself plunged into the flowing river. As before he felt no distress, in spite of the strangeness of the experience.

Ahead of him darted a fish, following the current. Encased by rock, the river flowed swiftly onward. At one point it briefly opened into a partially flooded cavern, before sweeping into a new passageway. Phosphorescence brightened some sections of the rock, but it was gone too quickly for him to properly take it in.

Apart from the fish leading him onward, he saw no living creature of any kind. Suddenly tumbling over a waterfall into a new underground cavern, they once more raced forward, finally bursting out of the rock and into the open. The river continued on its journey to the sea, but Dalthinir seemed to drift away from it.

HE WOKE with a start to find himself in the dark as before. Sitting up, he struggled to make sense of what he had just experienced. The dream—or was it a vision?—was clear in his memory. What did it mean? Was it a sign—something intended to stir him to action?

He pondered the first journey, upward to open sky. Perhaps there was a way out to the top of the cliffs. Even if it were true though, he couldn't see how it was useful to him. Quite apart from the fact that he didn't have wings, there was no way his body would fit in some of the cracks the moth had passed through. And what would he do if he found himself at the top of the cliff? How could he possibly climb down safely?

As for the dragon, everything he had been taught led him to believe that the creatures were extinct. The notion that one of them was napping in the cliffs beside the capital city of Periton was beyond absurd.

The more he thought about it, the less sense he could make of the journey upward. Could it have been symbolic? If its purpose had been to awaken his hope, it had fallen well short of the mark.

The second journey was almost as bizarre. If the dream in any way resembled reality, the river had carved out a passage large enough to easily admit a creature the size of an adult human. It might provide a way of escape if he had gills that allowed him to breathe underwater.

He had no way of being certain that a river even existed, but the least he could do was to find out.

Heading for the trickle of water that he had come to rely on, he used his elements magic to create a small ball of fire. He used its illumination to examine the rock.

He saw nothing to confirm the existence of a river. Placing his ear against the rock, he strained to hear any hint of the passage of water. He heard nothing.

More disheartened than ever, he sat down and allowed the ball of fire to wink out.

After what might have been an hour, he decided he'd been hungry and miserable for long enough. His situation might well be hopeless, but he had to at least try to do something.

Although his ability to move objects magically hadn't allowed him to dig himself out, his goal on this occasion was more modest. After igniting another ball of fire to give him some light, he stood well back from the section of rock where the water was trickling out. He pictured the location where he had gone through the rock in his dream. Then he magically picked up a boulder from the rubble left behind by

Banadin's rockfall and sent it smashing into the rock where the river should be. The rock wall remained intact, so he repeated the exercise, this time with a larger boulder.

On the fifth attempt, he was delighted to see a large hole in the wall. His excitement grew when he heard the unmistakable sound of rushing water.

Hurrying to the hole, he leaned over and peered in. A river was indeed flowing swiftly below the new opening he had created.

Now that he had access to the river, could he find a way to catch fish? He quickly pushed the idea from his mind. Access to a food supply might extend his life, but it wouldn't free him from his prison.

His magical abilities allowed him to form shields of different kinds. It occurred to him he could enter the river after magically wrapping himself inside a waterproof bubble to protect him from drowning.

The problem was that an effective bubble would be airtight as well as waterproof. And it would hold a limited amount of air.

He tried to remember what he'd seen in the dream. There had been at least one point where the river passed through an only partially flooded chamber. That should mean fresh air. He could open the bubble to refresh the stale air at that point. The key question was whether he would have enough air to last until then.

A bigger issue was whether the dream could be trusted at all. If the river continued underground instead of emerging into the open, before long he would suffocate.

After hesitating for a very long time, he acknowledged he was being foolish. What did he have to lose? If he remained in the cavern he would starve. A tiny chance of survival had to be better than no chance at all.

Climbing into the hole he readied himself to jump into the river. The first step was to form a waterproof bubble that would enclose him completely while stretching out behind him. A longer bubble should allow more air to be trapped inside. The second step was to add a layer of protection to the bubble to shield him from being battered against the rocks that formed the channel through which he must pass.

As soon as his protective bubble was ready, he jumped.

Hitting the water hard, his bubble was immediately caught by the current. He plunged forward, jostled back and forth between the walls of the channel.

The experience was terrifying. Swept along helplessly, he had no idea where he was going or where his journey would end. Brief hints of phosphorescence flashed by, but any similarity with the dream ended there. Everything was dark this time, and the calm detachment he felt before was a distant memory.

After being dragged along for some time he began to feel light-headed. It took him a while to grasp the significance of it, but when he did he began to sweat. He was running out of air.

If he could take the dream seriously, there would be another cavern at some point. But he could see nothing. How would he know when he reached it? Would he even be conscious by then? Panic rose up, threatening to overwhelm him. His eyelids began to sag, and his mind drifted lazily.

All of a sudden he began to slow. No longer bouncing off the rock sides of the channel, he was bobbing up and down in his little cocoon. Then it hit him. He must be floating in the cavern.

Did he dare risk opening his bubble? If he was wrong, water would sweep in, and he would drown.

The moments dragged by as he wavered. Then, aware his opportunity must surely come to an end soon, he tentatively opened a hole in the top of his bubble, ready to seal it in a moment if the need arose.

To his profound relief, nothing rushed in except air. Gasping it gratefully into his lungs, he felt his head clear immediately. At that moment, he began picking up speed again. He had barely sealed the bubble before he was again being propelled through a narrow channel, bumping from one side to the other.

The journey dragged on. Once more he felt his mind wandering. Keeping his eyes open became almost impossible. He vaguely recalled that something important was about to happen, but bringing it to mind was too much of an effort.

Suddenly he felt weightless. Relaxing, he allowed his eyes to fully close.

The experience ended with a bone-jarring crash, shocking him awake. He had just been plunged over a waterfall.

This time he didn't hesitate to open his bubble. Once more fresh air poured in to restore his senses before he sealed the opening.

The dream was proving prophetic. He had traveled only a short distance when he emerged into open air. It was nighttime. Crickets were chirping, the stars winked brightly, and moonlight reflected off the surface of the river. Dissolving his protective bubble, he struck out weakly for the riverbank and dragged himself ashore.

With the tension released at last, he began shivering uncontrollably. Try as he might, he couldn't blot out the horror of his underground tomb. He lay beside the river shaking like a leaf in the wind.

Eventually he was able to recover himself. Wincing from his bruises, he rolled onto his back and gazed up at the brilliant display above him. The heavens had not changed. Constant in their wonder and mystery, they remained entirely unperturbed by the trials and tribulations visited upon humankind.

Battered and bruised as he was after his unlikely escape, he had survived. He was alive thanks to a dream.

The ways of Providence were inscrutable. And yet he could not escape the conviction that there had been purpose behind his rescue. There were things he needed to do. He couldn't guess at everything that might be involved, although one task was immediately obvious. Banadin needed to be exposed.

CHAPTER 3

Dalthinir woke to bright sunlight with birds chirping cheerfully in the trees around him.

He found himself stretched out beside the embers of a fire he barely remembered setting. Having gone to sleep in his clothes, he was grateful to find them dry. His cloak was still hanging on the branch where he had left it. It appeared to have dried overnight as well.

His bruises felt even more uncomfortable than they had the previous night, although they were competing with hunger pangs for his attention. Climbing unsteadily to his feet, he tried to determine where he was.

His best guess placed him northwest of the city. No obvious signs of cultivation were visible, although farms must surely be located somewhere nearby.

Farms meant food, but they also meant further delays. Other mages back in the capital must surely be starting to feel concerned about him. He'd gone this long without food; he could last a few more hours. Using the position of the sun as a guide, he set off in what he hoped was a southeasterly direction, heading directly for Cambrick.

The sun had passed its zenith when he reached a dirt road that seemed to be heading in roughly the right direction. Less than an hour later a cart approached him, heading in the opposite direction.

The driver of the cart stopped when he reached him.

"Are you returning from the market?" asked Dalthinir.

The farmer nodded. "You heading that way yourself?"

"I am. I imagine it will be a long walk."

The farmer nodded a confirmation. "I'm returning to the farm. Seems like my cured pork is in high demand. If you're still walking when I return, I'll give you a ride."

Dalthinir nodded gratefully. "Thank you. I'll take you up on your offer."

Feeling his exhaustion keenly, he sat down under a tree by the side of the road.

The farmer eyed him sympathetically. "Why don't you join me now? It isn't far, and I'd welcome the company."

The mage needed no urging. Climbing up beside the driver, he sat down gratefully.

They rolled forward in silence for a while. "You look a little the worse for wear," the farmer finally ventured.

Having already decided not to speak of his ordeal before he was with the chief master, Dalthinir deflected the question. "I fell into a river and was carried downstream for a way."

"You look a bit pinched. I'm guessing you haven't eaten for a while."

"It's true," he acknowledged.

"We'll sort you out before we head back to Cambrick," the farmer promised.

Dalthinir nodded gratefully. Nodding was, in fact, becoming hard to avoid as they bounced along. The further they went, the more of it he was doing. Perhaps the hour had been late when he'd crawled onto the riverbank the previous night. Perhaps he was simply exhausted. Either way, he wasn't finding it easy to stay awake.

As soon as they reached their destination, the farmer bustled him into the farmhouse and sat him at a table. Soon fresh milk, cheese, salted pork, and thick slices of bread appeared before him. He stared at it wide-eyed before setting to with new-found energy.

When he finished, he pushed outside to find the farmer had been loading the wagon while he ate. After lending a hand to complete the process, he climbed up beside the farmer once more and they set off.

He'd been too weary to notice on the way in, but the road used by the farmer wound around a hill with steep slopes. At one point a small landslide had buried the road, forcing the farmer to drive the cart well out of its way over rough ground. As they approached, Dalthinir saw a way to repay the farmer's kindness.

"Can you stop here, please?" he asked as they approached the area.

The farmer looked at him curiously for a moment, then he pulled the cart to a halt. As the two men watched, the earth and rocks from the slide began to move, disappearing over the edge on the other side of the road. The process continued until the road was completely clear.

The farmer had watched in awe. "I saw from the crimson edging on your cloak that you were a mage," he said. "But I've never seen anything like that! How did you do it?"

"My magical ability allows me to move things. I wanted to thank you for your help."

"You may consider any debt more than repaid!" the farmer assured him. "It would have taken me and several of my workers many hours to do what you just achieved in a few minutes!"

They followed the newly cleared road for only a few minutes before the farmer stopped the cart again. "Why don't you climb in back with my pork?" he suggested. "You'll fall off if you stay up here for much longer!"

Dalthinir readily followed his suggestion.

He woke to find the farmer calling to him. "The gates of Cambrick are ahead. Where would you like me to drop you?"

"I'm heading for my quarters. It's in one of the buildings occupied by the Compact."

"I'll take you there as soon as I've delivered this pork."

With Dalthinir's help, the unloading didn't take long. The cart soon arrived at the Compact building where his quarters were located.

"Thank you," he called to the farmer.

"My pleasure! Stop by anytime," the farmer called back as he drove away.

Dalthinir heaved a sigh of relief. He was home, unattainable as that had seemed twenty four hours earlier. The first thing he intended to do was to change his torn and soiled garments. Then he would seek out the chief master.

Turning toward his quarters, he came face to face with Inga. The breeze was playing with her black hair, and her cheeks seemed rosier than ever.

"You're back already!" she said brightly.

He looked at her blankly. "What do you mean?"

"Are your family well? I heard that you urgently needed to visit them for a few days."

"Who told you that?"

Her brows furrowed. "I'm not entirely sure." She took a step back, looking at him as if she was only just registering his appearance. "What happened to you?"

"I'm fortunate to be alive," he told her seriously.

Her face creased in concern. "You had an accident?"

"It was no accident," he assured her. "Someone tried to kill me."

Her shocked face stared up at him. "Who would do such a thing?"

"Our own Master Banadin," he replied bitterly. "I imagine he's the source of the story about me being out of town unexpectedly."

She stood gaping at him.

"I mustn't talk about it. Not until I've spoken to Chief Master Sentaris."

"I won't detain you. But I want you to promise me you'll tell me everything that happened!"

He nodded, then hurried inside. His heart sank when he realized that in his distraction he'd failed to pay her any more than the most cursory attention. He hadn't even thanked her for her concern. He could only hope there would be an opportunity to mend it later.

As soon as he was vaguely presentable, he hurried to the quarters of Chief Master Sentaris.

The head mage was in his quarters, as had increasingly been the case in recent times. He was conversing with Master Adrastas, a budding administrator who seemed likely to one day succeed the aging chief master.

"Master Dalthinir!" said the head mage brightly. "It is good to see you. I heard you were out of town unexpectedly at short notice. Is everything well with you?"

"Not at all, Chief Master. I have been through a very difficult experience."

The chief master raised his eyebrows. "Please, take a seat."

"I decided a few days ago to keep an eye on Master Banadin."

"Whatever for?" asked Master Adrastas in surprise.

"It was prompted by a conversation I had with Lord Platten."

"The one who was killed because he had an affair?"

"Yes. He said that Banadin tried to recruit him for a scheme that he described as nefarious. Using magic to overturn the established order. He said it was dangerous nonsense, and he refused to have anything to do with it. Two days later he was dead."

"Are you suggesting that Master Banadin was involved in some way?" Adrastas looked skeptical.

"Not directly. But someone sent an anonymous letter tipping off the wronged husband."

"And you decided that Banadin did it?"

"I concluded that it was possible. If Lord Platten was to be believed, Banadin had a reason to want him silenced."

"This is a serious matter! Do you have any proof that this conversation between the two of them took place?" asked Adrastas.

"None whatever. But I knew Lord Platten for many years, and he was not known to embellish the truth."

"So you decided to keep an eye on Master Banadin. You do realize that what you did was an invasion of his privacy?"

"I never violated his privacy. I discovered he was spending considerable time individually with several other mages—Masters Roza, Garmer, Clarree, Petria, and Lars—but I made no attempt to listen in on their conversations."

"Even tracking people is crossing a line," asserted Adrastas. "Like all of us, you took an oath never to use your magical abilities to benefit yourself at the expense of others."

Dalthinir might have seen it the same way if Banadin had done nothing wrong. But any misgivings had melted away when the man tried to kill him.

"I wasn't doing any of it to benefit myself. Lord Platten only died after Banadin crossed a much more serious line when speaking with him. I couldn't just ignore it."

"Please continue with your story," suggested the chief master.

"I followed Banadin to a location in the cliff at the rear of the city. I found a tunnel going into the cliff and followed it in. Inside I found a desk with a number of forbidden texts, along with Master Banadin's seal and letters bearing his name."

"They could have been placed there by anyone," interjected Adrastas.

Dalthinir nodded. "That is true. Except while I was there Banadin himself arrived. I hid when I heard him coming. After he had cleared away all the evidence, he made a little speech to the person who had come snooping on him. As you know, he doesn't sense magical auras, so he didn't know who I was. He said that he had enjoyed his little haven, but it was time to move on. He hoped I would enjoy it as much as he did, because I would never be leaving it. He then precipitated a massive rockfall that left me trapped in the cavern."

"Why didn't you use your own abilities to move the rocks out of the way?"

"I tried, but it led to an even bigger rockfall."

"Then how did you escape?"

Dalthinir quickly decided that talking about the dream might raise more questions than it answered. "After being trapped in there for a couple of days, I became quite despairing. But I managed to find a way out using an underground river. I was able to wrap myself in a protective bubble and ride it out of the cliffs."

The chief master's face was expressionless. "That's quite a story, Dalthinir!"

"I am willing to take Master Adrastas to the location. The tunnel is blocked on the inside, but it should be possible to verify its existence."

"I am willing to go with you on one condition," Adrastas replied.

"What condition is that?"

"That you repeat your story in front of Master Banadin. These are serious allegations, Dalthinir! An accused person has a right to face their accuser."

Dalthinir nodded. "I am certainly willing to do that."

"In that case I propose we leave immediately."

The two of them made their way across the city to the location of the tunnel. It took some time to get there, and when they did Dalthinir hunted around for many minutes before he found the place. By then Adrastas was becoming noticeably impatient.

Dalthinir hadn't recognized the location because the house had been demolished completely. And when he examined the cliff face, he saw that a significant rockslide had buried every trace of the tunnel.

"This is where it was. But there's been a rockslide, and the house has been demolished."

Adrastas didn't appear impressed. "In the last two or three days?"

"Certainly. It wasn't like this when I came here."

A rough-looking man had been watching them curiously.

Adrastas noticed him. "Do you live nearby?"

The man nodded. "Aye."

"Was there a rockslide here recently?"

The man shook his head firmly. "It's been like that for years."

Dalthinir stared at him with narrowed eyes. The man must have been bribed. Banadin had told Dalthinir he'd had the tunnel watched. This man was probably the person he paid to do it.

Adrastas had seen more than enough.

"You will be facing Master Banadin first thing in the morning. Make sure you're prepared. I'd strongly suggest you come with something more solid than what you've presented so far."

With that he marched off. After a glare at Banadin's man, Dalthinir followed him.

With no remaining trace of the tunnel, Dalthinir had been robbed of any hope of corroborating even the smallest part of his story. It was becoming obvious that Banadin had covered his tracks very effectively.

He faced the uncomfortable truth—his account was going to seem far-fetched to any impartial observer.

Returning home gloomy and frustrated, Dalthinir was intercepted by Master Inga. "I want to hear your story," she told him. Seeing his less than enthusiastic response, she added, "You promised, remember?"

He shrugged helplessly.

Taking him in hand, she steered him to a quiet location and sat him down, positioning herself opposite.

"You're clearly troubled, Dalthinir!" she began. "I want to hear everything that's happened. From the beginning."

He was hesitant at first, but after his experience with Adrastas it was difficult to resist a sympathetic ear. Once he started, it all came pouring out. He held nothing back, not even the dream.

She gave him her full attention. From time to time she asked questions for clarification. Otherwise she remained silent.

When he had finished, she shook her head in wonder. "That is a remarkable story. Your escape was truly extraordinary. And the dream is fascinating. It seems unlikely you would have survived without it."

"What do you make of the dragon?" he asked.

"I'm not sure. It's baffling. Perhaps it was somehow symbolic."

He shrugged. "You may be right. I'm not sure what it might symbolize though."

She looked him in the eyes. "I believe you, Dalthinir. I want you to know that."

"Even though I have no evidence to offer? Evidence means everything to Adrastas and the chief master. I'm not sure either of them believed a word I said."

"They have evidence. It's readily visible to anyone with eyes to see it! Your character is compelling evidence. Anyone who knows you will agree you're a remarkably straightforward person. You speak the truth when it doesn't benefit you to do so, and I've consistently found you to be a person of integrity. Even without hard evidence to support your story, your character lends considerable weight to your words."

"Thank you, Inga. That means a great deal." He raised an eyebrow. "If it isn't inappropriate to ask, I'm curious to know how you would characterize our Master Banadin."

She looked uncomfortable. "It isn't my practice to speak ill of others behind their backs. These are exceptional circumstances, though. While acknowledging that Master Banadin is a clever man and a powerful mage, I also see him as a person with hidden agendas. I don't always find it easy to know when to take what he says at face value."

Dalthinir sighed. "I can only hope that the chief master and his deputy are equally insightful. I cannot pretend I'm optimistic."

CHAPTER 4

Dalthinir's meeting with the chief master, Master Adrastas, and Master Banadin hadn't been going well.

Banadin's face was twisted in fury. "So you admit you've been snooping on me and my friends?"

"I was following you," Dalthinir returned, trying to sound more unruffled than he felt. Apparently Banadin had been made aware that Dalthinir had tracked his meetings with other mages.

The accused mage jabbed a finger at Dalthinir. "This imbecile is one of the few mages capable of detecting magical auras. He's undeserving of the ability." He rounded on Chief Master Sentaris. "We cannot condone mages using their abilities to violate their oaths for the sake of pursuing personal vendettas. Such behavior *must* be sanctioned!"

When the chief master made no comment, Banadin turned to Dalthinir again. "And you claim I am responsible for the death of Lord Platten?"

"I have merely repeated what he told me two days before his murder. The outcome of your conversation with him gives you a motive."

"There is no motive, because no such conversation ever happened," stated Banadin coldly. "As for your nonsensical claims about me trapping you underground, you haven't even been able to show Master Adrastas the place where it supposedly happened. The obvious conclusion is that you lost touch with reality for a couple of days. Sad as that may be, it does not excuse the offensive accusations you have been making."

Dalthinir glared at him. "If I am making this up, who spread the highly convenient rumor that I was away from the city visiting family?"

"You probably spread the rumor yourself in an effort to cover your lapse!"

Banadin confronted the aging Sentaris, his hands raised in a gesture of angry frustration. "What are you planning to do, Chief Master? This fool comes spouting accusations that can only tarnish the reputation of his fellow mages, yet he offers no evidence to support any of them. Are you going to allow him to continue doing it without suffering consequences of any kind?"

However he might seem to the others, Dalthinir was greatly disheartened. His case sounded unconvincing even to his own ears.

The meeting ended with nothing resolved. But Dalthinir had the feeling that the chief master and Adrastas saw him as extremely fortunate that no action had been taken against him. It was infuriating that Banadin, after leaving him to die, could so deftly turn it all around by blaming the victim. The man's reputation for cunning was well deserved.

The following day Dalthinir stepped outside his quarters to be confronted by Master Garmer.

"How dare you take it upon yourself to monitor my whereabouts?" spat the mage. "You won't get away with it!"

It wasn't long before he encountered Master Roza. She looked like she was ready to scratch his eyes out. "You deserve to be thrown out of the Compact after your baseless accusations!"

He hurried away only to come face to face with Master Clarree. "You'll pay for what you've done!" he growled.

As the day progressed he noticed other mages eyeing him curiously. A few looked away as soon as he glanced in their direction. Banadin had clearly been busy applying sanctions of his own.

That night he slept poorly, too distracted to settle easily. From all appearances, Banadin was going to get away with attempted murder, to say nothing of his likely role in the death of Lord Platten. But what could Dalthinir do?

It came as no surprise that Banadin's closest associates had turned on his accuser. Yet the strength of their vitriol seemed out of proportion. It suggested to him they had something to hide. There seemed little doubt that Banadin had drawn them into his forbidden pursuits, although it brought him little comfort to recognize it.

He felt alone and helpless. Were there others who perceived the fury of Banadin's close associates as manufactured? What was the man up to, and where would it end?

The following morning Inga sought him out.

"I think you could use a distraction, Dalthinir," she said, gazing at him with concern in her eyes. "I'm about to have my midday meal with Emmela. Please come and join us."

He readily agreed. Emmela might not have been his first choice, but he did need something else to focus on.

Emmela was different from Inga in many ways, but they were good friends. He had always perceived Emmela as a person who liked neat answers. In her view, something was either right or it was wrong—she didn't cope well with ambiguity. It seemed ironic since her magical ability was illusion.

She was also a straight talker.

"You seem to have upset a few people, Dalthinir," she said the moment he arrived.

Inga frowned. "I brought him here to give him a break from all of that."

Emmela was unmoved. "Your concern for others truly is admirable, Inga. I've always said so. But caring about people isn't a reason to ignore what's going on around you."

"What's going on around Inga that she can't ignore, Emmela?" he asked.

"Well, since you ask, I'm hearing that you have been tracking the whereabouts of other mages without official approval. Is that true?"

"What gives you the right to ask me that?"

"I have a right to know if my privacy has been breached!"

"I can assure you I have never tracked your whereabouts, with or without official approval. Are you satisfied?"

"No, I am not! You haven't denied doing it to others! I've also heard you're accusing Master Banadin of trying to murder you. That's a serious charge. None of us has the right to slur our fellow mages."

"It isn't a slur if it's true."

"If it's true then call for him to be tried."

"What if I can't prove it?"

"Then you have no grounds for accusing him!"

"Even if he did try to kill me?"

"You clearly don't look like you've been murdered. You don't even appear to be injured!"

"So you're willing to believe whatever people are saying, just because they say it?"

"People don't say things like this without a reason."

He shrugged. "On that point we're in complete agreement. They certainly have their reasons for saying what they're saying."

Inga had gone red in the face. "That's enough!" she exclaimed. "I am hosting this meal, and I refuse to allow further conversation about such matters."

Emmela subsided dutifully, and Dalthinir certainly had no reason to continue the conversation.

In spite of energetic efforts by Inga to change the tone, the meal was not relaxing for any of them. After another hour had passed, Dalthinir decided he could respectably find an excuse to slip away.

Before he could do anything, one of the Compact's maids burst into the room breathlessly.

"Have you heard the news?!" she panted. Noticing belatedly that Dalthinir was present, she suddenly became awkward. "I...I believe the chief master is looking for you," she told him.

"What's your news?" he asked.

"Master Banadin is dead!" she replied.

"When did it happen?"

"Just now! Someone was with him until only half an hour ago."

"And why does Chief Master Sentaris want me?"

"Master Clarree and Master Roza are claiming that you murdered him! They're calling for you to be tried."

Dalthinir turned to Emmela. "It must be true," he said.

She frowned. "What are you talking about? If he died in the last half hour, it's obvious you couldn't have done it. You've been here with us for much longer than that."

"But you said it yourself," he told her. "People don't say things like this without a reason."

She frowned down at her plate.

"Thank you for a delicious meal and for your thoughtfulness, Master Inga. If you will both excuse me, it seems I have an unexpected appointment with Chief Master Sentaris," he said.

After bowing briefly, he left.

DALTHINIR FOUND the chief master with Adrastas. Both of them looked surprised when he appeared.

"I believe you are looking for me, Chief Master."

The head mage looked pale and worn. "Ah, Master Dalthinir. Yes. Thank you for turning yourself in."

"Is that what I'm doing?"

"Well we do need to follow due process. Master Banadin is dead, and it has been suggested that you had a clear interest in the matter. I am not saying you killed him, of course. Your trial hasn't happened yet. But it seems reasonable to believe you had a motive."

"Because he tried to kill me?"

"Because you claim he tried to kill you," corrected Adrastas.

Dalthinir smiled, although there was no humor in it. "You suspect that I murdered Banadin in revenge. In revenge for what? That motive only makes sense if he tried to murder me, which you don't believe. The truth is much stranger. He did try to murder me, yet I had no involvement—direct or indirect—in his death."

They had no immediate response.

"Can I ask how he died?"

Adrastas considered a moment before answering. "His cause of death is not easy to determine."

Dalthinir nodded slowly. "Having caught a glimpse of what he was dabbling in, I can imagine that almost anything was possible."

"Where were you in the last hour?" asked Adrastas.

"I was enjoying a midday meal with Master Inga and Master Emmela," he replied.

Adrastas and the chief master exchanged sharp glances.

"For that entire period?"

He nodded.

"Will they confirm that?"

"They will," he replied. "You will, of course, ask them yourselves, as you should." He gave another wry smile. "If you do a minimum of digging, you will discover that Master Emmela is not an enthusiastic supporter of mine. It's therefore ironic that she should be the one to offer me an alibi. Perhaps it's fortuitous for me though. No one could credibly accuse her of lying on my behalf."

Neither of them offered comment.

"So you've promised to offer me up as a sacrifice to Banadin's supporters. When is this trial to begin?"

Adrastas didn't hesitate. "As soon as possible. If you were where you claim to be, the trial will be over quickly."

"May I ask what evidence prompted the trial?"

Again they were silent.

He shook his head slowly. "So you agreed to a trial without my accusers having offered even a shred of evidence. If I hadn't been so fortunate with my alibi, would you have convicted me without evidence?"

"Any such insinuation is insulting," growled Adrastas.

"Is it?" asked Dalthinir, his eyes on the unmistakable blush covering the face of Chief Master Sentaris.

He turned back to Master Adrastas. "You came close to sanctioning me for accusing Banadin without evidence. Yet you were willing to try me for murder on the basis of nothing more than a chorus of complaints."

The chief master finally found his voice. "If it's justice you're looking for, then you have a strange way of recommending yourself to those who will be handing it out."

"Mages expect you to serve justice solely on the merits of the case. Not because an accused party ingratiates themselves with you, nor because others badger you. I hope you will not disappoint us."

"Unbiased justice is what you can expect," said the chief master. Dalthinir noted he was still faintly blushing.

"Am I free to go, or am I to be detained pending this trial?"

Adrastas opened his mouth, but the chief master got in first. "Given the circumstances I will not detain you. I am sure I do not need to tell you to remain in Cambrick until after the trial is over. We will try to organize it promptly, so you will not be kept waiting for long."

"Thank you, Chief Master. I appreciate your gesture."

"I think it might be wise, Chief Master, if we sent a person or two along with him. They can accompany him until after the trial. The situation needs to be taken seriously. We don't want to set precedents we might later regret."

Sentaris sighed. He looked spent. "Very well, Adrastas. If you think that's necessary. But they can tail him. They don't have to march along on either side of him as if he's a convicted criminal."

Adrastas looked as if he might considering arguing. If so, he changed his mind.

"If you would be willing to wait a few minutes," Sentaris concluded, "Master Adrastas will arrange for someone suitable to follow you."

In the end, Dalthinir waited a couple of hours.

At one point while he was waiting, the chief master came and sank into a chair beside him. Heaving a sigh, he passed a hand over his face. "I'm sorry about all this, Dalthinir. I know I've allowed myself to be pushed and pulled a little too much in recent times. The truth is I'm very weary. I don't have the fight I once did."

Dalthinir looked at him in concern. "Are you being properly cared for, Chief Master? You don't look well."

Sentaris waved a hand dismissively. "I just need some rest. I'm planning to lie down as soon as I leave. Adrastas can handle anything else that's needed."

He rose to his feet with difficulty. Before leaving, he bent down and said, "I don't believe you killed him, Dalthinir!"

"Thank you, Chief Master," he managed.

He watched, frowning, as Sentaris hobbled away, wishing he had at least a minimum of medical skill to offer.

It was becoming increasingly clear that his fate lay in the hands of Adrastas.

HEADING BACK TO HIS QUARTERS, Dalthinir tried not to dwell on the fact that two mages were tailing him. They were at least keeping their distance. He had the aging chief master to thank for that.

As he drew near his building, he passed a broken down wagon. Four men were kneeling around one of the wheels. As he passed, three of them sprang up with clubs in their hands and attacked him.

He barely managed to put a shield in place before they were raining blows on him. Thankfully they were unable to hurt him.

His own options were limited. Mages were strictly forbidden from using magic against any other person, mage or non-mage. But the constraints were particularly rigorous in the case of non-magical people, given their relative helplessness.

Before he could decide what to do, one of the men dropped his club and held his head, wailing, "This mage attacked me! He tried to suffocate me with magic!" Within moments, the other two had copied him. He noticed their clubs being retrieved and hidden by the other man with the wagon.

At that moment, Master Lars appeared.

"Stop attacking those men immediately!" he demanded, stabbing a finger at Dalthinir.

The two mages sent by Adrastas hurried forward.

"The only attack here has been on Master Dalthinir," one of them told Master Lars curtly. "It should have been obvious to you that he used power only to shield himself. Move on!"

Lars scowled at the rebuke, but he disappeared promptly enough. Every mage was capable of detecting the use of magical power—that ability was the characteristic that identified a person as a mage—so Lars could have been in no doubt of the truth. He clearly hadn't expected to encounter witnesses who could exonerate Dalthinir.

Other mages had arrived in response to the scuffle, and Dalthinir's protectors arranged for them to escort the four men away for questioning.

Adrastas's mages walked beside Dalthinir as he continued toward his quarters.

"That scene was carefully planned," Dalthinir told them grimly. "If those men were unable to harm me, they were ready to implicate me in an attack on non-mages."

His companions didn't offer comment, although he had the impression they agreed with him.

"One of us will report back to Master Adrastas," they told him. "The other will take watch outside your quarters."

"Through the night?" he asked.

They nodded.

"In that case you might as well come inside. I have a couch in the front room one of you can sleep on. It's right beside the front door, so you'll know if I try to leave. And in case my word means anything to you, I promise I will not make an attempt to slip away from you before the trial."

After exchanging glances, they nodded. "Thank you for your offer. A couch will be more comfortable than standing outside in the cold."

One of them left immediately to report to Adrastas. Night had fallen by the time he returned, but Dalthinir was still awake. He and the other mage had shared a meal.

"What did you learn about the men who attacked me?" asked Dalthinir curiously.

"I'm not sure how much I'm supposed to say," the mage answered cautiously. Then he shrugged. "They claimed it was a case of mistaken identity. They thought you were Master Hamfisk."

"The mage accused of embezzling a non-mage family? He was acquitted, wasn't he?"

"Yes. The men are saying that justice was denied, so they decided to take it into their own hands."

Dalthinir rolled his eyes. "They had their story well prepared. What will happen to them?"

"They've been detained. They will be charged with assault."

"And Master Lars?"

"He says he happened to be passing by, and he took the situation at face value."

Dalthinir snorted. "The fact that he was one of Banadin's close confidants has nothing to do with it, of course."

With the evening drawing on, one of the mages settled onto the couch in Dalthinir's quarters. The other left for his own home, promising to return as soon as the sun rose.

It had been an eventful afternoon. Dalthinir had been unimpressed when Adrastas insisted on sending mages to accompany him. Now he was grateful for it.

CHAPTER 5

Any hope Dalthinir might have had of a prompt trial was dashed the following morning. When the other mage appeared at Dalthinir's quarters as promised, he reported that Sentaris was gravely ill. The chief master survived only until the following morning.

The funeral was a major event, with every mage attending. Dalthinir was among them, flanked by his two guards. The occasion was organized by Master Adrastas. Before the week was out he had been appointed as successor to Chief Master Sentaris.

Adrastas seemed to have forgotten entirely about Dalthinir's case. The new chief master had undoubtedly long since confirmed his alibi. He would therefore have been well aware that the trial would shed no light on Banadin's death. It came as no surprise to Dalthinir that dealing with the matter did not rank high on the long list of issues the new head mage needed to address.

As the days passed he continued in a state of uncertainty. Inga finally decided to intervene on his behalf. She accused the new chief master to his face of gross injustice in leaving a man with a criminal charge hanging over his head, shadowed by two guards everywhere he went. The more so since he knew as well as she did that Dalthinir was not guilty of the charge.

If Adrastas had little concern about Dalthinir's situation, he apparently cared about his image. A hearing was scheduled for two days later.

The Compact's auditorium was packed when proceedings got underway. Presiding over the trial, supported by a small panel of senior mages, Adrastas read the charges. "Master Dalthinir, you are charged with murdering Master Banadin. Do you accept or deny the charge?"

Dalthinir rose to his feet. "I deny the charge," he replied, ignoring taunts that rose above the murmurs rippling through the audience.

"A number of people have applied to bring evidence. Each of you will be heard. I will call Master Garmer first."

Master Garmer rose and stepped forward. "This man," he said, pointing an accusing finger at Dalthinir, "accused Master Banadin of attempted murder. He was unable to support his vicious slur with the tiniest shred of evidence. He attempted to tarnish the reputation of an honorable and respected member of the Compact. The two of them had similar magical abilities, but Dalthinir did not share Master Banadin's ability to magically understand other languages, human and non-human. It is clear that the murderer before us was eaten up with envy. When his slur had no impact, he had the presumption to end Master Banadin's life! He does not deserve to live!"

The murmuring was louder this time. Adrastas waited for it to die down. "What evidence can you present to support your accusation of murder?" he asked.

"The evidence I have already presented is clear and compelling!" retorted Garmer.

"You have addressed nothing beyond the question of motive," corrected Adrastas stiffly. "If you have no actual evidence to offer in support of your accusations, I will call the next witness."

Master Roza stepped up next. After delivering more of the same, she added, "This man not only murdered Master Banadin, he abused his ability to trace glimmer. He admitted to Chief Master Adrastas that he has snooped on other mages, including myself. All of it was done in a futile effort to build a case against Master Banadin. He violated his oath never to use his magical abilities to benefit himself at the expense of others. He cannot be allowed to continue such abuses!"

Master Clarree threw more fuel onto the same fire. "No mage with the ability to track magical auras can be allowed to turn their farsense against other mages! It is intolerable! After the way he has violated our privacy, many mages, myself included, no longer feel safe with this man in our midst. He has engaged in conduct unbecoming a member of the Compact. Such behavior must be sanctioned!"

Loud muttering accompanied these remarks.

Adrastas had heard enough from Dalthinir's accusers. He called Master Inga forward. "What evidence do you have that is relevant to this case?"

"On the day Master Banadin died, I was having my midday meal when a maid rushed in and said she had come from a sensational announcement. Master Banadin had just been found dead, after being seen alive half an hour earlier."

"That is correct," confirmed the chief master. "I made that announcement myself."

"Then Master Dalthinir could not have killed him. He was eating with Master Emmela and me at the time, and he had been with us for well over an hour." She glared at Garmer and the others. "I find it incredible that people can accuse someone of murder with nothing more substantial than their own prejudices to base it on."

"Thank you, Master Inga," said Adrastas hastily, getting in before she could be shouted down. "Master Emmela?"

When Emmela came forward he asked, "Do you concur with Master Inga's evidence?"

"I do," she confirmed.

"Do you have anything further to add?"

"No," she said.

"We have heard enough," Adrastas asserted. "The panel will confer and return with a verdict."

They were gone for far longer than Dalthinir expected.

When they returned, Adrastas called for order. "Some will undoubtedly ask what prompted Master Sentaris to lay charges against Master Dalthinir in the first place. He did so only because of

Master Dalthinir's unsubstantiated claims that Master Banadin tried to murder him. These accusations might have suggested the existence of a motive to do some kind of mischief to Master Banadin. However, based on the clear evidence of Masters Inga and Emmela, we find Master Dalthinir not guilty of the murder of Master Banadin."

He faced Dalthinir. "You are free to go. However, I have a couple of statements to make first. On behalf of the panel I wish to convey our deep concern at you having made serious accusations against Master Banadin you were unable to support. We also reluctantly find it necessary to sanction you for invading the privacy of other mages by tracking them without authorization. From now on, you are not permitted to use your farsense to track magical glimmer without official permission."

He turned back to the room, ignoring the sensation created by his words. "I hereby pronounce this hearing closed!" he yelled over the din.

Dalthinir remained where he was, numbed by the panel's sanction. Although most of the mages filed past without comment on their way out of the building, he was subjected to a torrent of abuse from a vocal minority. A couple of mages even spat on him.

Master Inga appeared, and planted herself before him with hands on her hips, glaring at anyone who as much as hesitated on their way past.

Adrastas was among the last to leave. Dalthinir came to life as he passed.

"Chief Master! You publicly berated me for bringing accusations against Banadin without proof. I did so in private. Masters Clarree, Garmer, and Roza subjected me to the same thing, but in public. Yet you did nothing to call them to account for their behavior."

Adrastas had nothing to say.

"The prohibition you placed on me seems little more than an attempt to appease a vocal minority. I appeal to you to lift it."

The chief master's eyes narrowed. "I have nothing further to say." With that he turned on his heel and left the building.

As he left, Dalthinir noticed that Lars had been lurking near the doorway. If the smirk on his face gave any indication, he had clearly witnessed the interaction.

Inga had heard it too. "I don't think Chief Master Adrastas is going to thank you for pointing out his inconsistencies." She peered at him with concern in her eyes. "It could have been worse. You have your freedom, and your name has been cleared."

"You can hardly say my name has been cleared!" he retorted. "I've been cautioned for supposedly bringing false accusations against Banadin, and sanctioned for tracking his movements."

Seeing the impact of his outburst on her, he quickly apologized. "I'm sorry, Inga. I know you're only trying to help. Right now the future seems very bleak for me."

His comment about the future seemed to dishearten her for reasons he didn't understand. Nodding tightly, she left him to his ruminations.

Delighted to be setting out on his own again, he reached his quarters without incident. But as time passed, appearing in public became increasingly unpleasant. Banadin's close circle took every opportunity to abuse him, and many other mages turned away when they saw him approach. If was almost worse when people didn't turn away, because he never knew whether to expect insults or sympathetic smiles from them.

He hadn't forgotten the incident beside the wagon either. Shielding himself would not be enough in such a situation. He needed mage witnesses if he was to avoid false accusations. He looked back longingly on the period when guards had been tailing him.

As the days passed, he felt increasingly alone.

He had never seen himself as an angry or vindictive person, but every day now he wrestled with dark daydreams at the expense of his oppressors. He had obvious reason to be angry with Clarree and Roza and their collaborators, but he was also frustrated with Adrastas for what he perceived as failures of justice at his expense. A number of his fellow mages had also turned against him for no good reason.

Even Inga seemed to be keeping her distance, which baffled and disheartened him. He wondered if she had given up on him.

• • •

Two things happened that changed his perspective completely.

The first was a visit to a farm.

After they completed their training, most mages spent a proportion of their time using their magical abilities to support agriculture or one or other of the guilds. The payment they received funded their living costs. Dalthinir was included in their number. His ability to move objects, to manipulate the elements, and even to provide protective shields, made him useful for a range of projects.

Other mages chose not to actively involve themselves in such pursuits. A few who were independently wealthy, such as the late Master Banadin, enjoyed considerable freedom to use their time and their magical abilities in whatever ways they chose.

The magical abilities of some mages had little practical application in industry. Master Inga, whose sole ability was to detect magical auras and the use of magical power over a considerable distance, was one example. Master Emmela, whose ability involved illusion, was another.

Mages like Inga and Emmela generally supported themselves in other ways. Emmela, along with a number of others, had a role interacting with farmers and tradespeople who came to the Compact seeking magical assistance. She had become skilled at tracking down available mages with suitable abilities. Inga was involved in Compact administration.

On that particular day, Emmela had approached Dalthinir with a request to assist a farmer in time-critical repairs to a dam. "I thought you might benefit from an opportunity to get out of the city," she said gruffly.

Dalthinir thanked her sincerely. She was undoubtedly right about him needing a change of environment. Even if she had mixed motives for wanting him gone, she was doing him a favor.

He completed the farmer's task without difficulty. With the sun about to set, the farmer invited the mage to stay at the farmhouse overnight, promising to return him the following day. Dalthinir readily agreed.

The next morning he woke early and went for a walk. Just after dawn he witnessed a bird of prey swooping down on chicks in the farmyard. With the hens scattered by the raptor, a rooster raced in, ferociously attacking the predator. It harassed the larger bird so relentlessly that the intruder flew off in disarray.

The rooster's determination to protect the helpless chicks undoubtedly owed more to instinct than to reason, but it had shown complete disregard for its own safety.

The incident shook Dalthinir. It was clear that the bird had no certainty of success when it set out to defend the helpless chicks. Yet it hadn't hesitated.

He himself was an intelligent and accomplished person, but also one who had given in to self-pity. It was clearly time to stop allowing himself to be intimidated by the forces that opposed him.

The second event that spurred a change of perspective took place not long after his return from the farm. The maid that serviced his quarters arrived and set to work restoring order from the chaos. She liked to chatter while she was working if he was present.

"You and your mage friends must have a lot of business affairs to conduct," she said.

"What makes you say that?" he asked.

"One of my friends works for a member of the Notaries Guild, and she overhears all kinds of things. Like about the mage that died. Master Banadin, I think his name was."

She suddenly had Dalthinir's full attention.

"You would think that once Master Banadin was gone, that would be it. But he left instructions in the event of his death. Mountains of them! And things to distribute. Some now, and some in the future. The notary has been working harder than he'd ever needed to while the man was alive!"

"Bless you, Millie!" he said, and meant it.

The information was a revelation. He'd been fool enough to believe that Banadin's pursuits had died with him. But the man had gathered a following among the mages—they'd become Dalthinir's persecutors, so he had no difficulty naming each of them.

There was only one possible conclusion: Banadin had done everything necessary to ensure his forbidden activities would not cease in the event of his death.

Dalthinir had no proof, but he was certain of it. He was the only person outside Banadin's circle who understood what the mage had been involved in. But there was nothing he could do. Adrastas had banned him from monitoring Banadin's acolytes. They were free to do whatever they liked.

He'd told Inga. She was as capable of monitoring magical auras as he was. But he knew enough of her to know she wouldn't do it. She'd never been one to cross forbidden boundaries.

There was no point asking others to step in on his behalf anyway. He was the one with the knowledge, so it was his responsibility.

He was one man, and the forces arrayed against him were much stronger. But allowing himself to be intimidated was a choice. The rooster had shown him that.

Time passed, and life became no easier than it had been from the first day of his confrontation with Banadin. Masters Clarree, Roza, and Garmer, actively assisted by Petria and Lars, were succeeding in making his life a daily misery. Far too many other mages were following their lead in small ways that nevertheless had a cumulative effect. He began to doubt if it would ever be possible to return to the life he had known before Banadin trapped him underground.

When he took a step back to see beyond his own comfort, he saw that Banadin's followers had been using him to send a warning. They were ensuring that no one would dare pay close attention to them. Not when the personal cost was so high.

Monitoring Banadin's followers from within the Compact was now out of the question, however bold he might choose to be. Nothing prevented him from ignoring the Compact's ban, of course. He could use his farsense secretly and deny having done so. But he had never been good at pretending to be someone he was not.

A conviction began to grow within him. If he was free of the strictures placed upon him by the Compact, he could do what was necessary himself. Even from a distance.

The conclusion was inescapable. For him to carry out what he believed his responsibilities to be, he would need to embrace the unthinkable. He would need to leave the Compact.

He would need to become a renegade.

CHAPTER 6

Finally mustering the courage to do what he should have done much sooner, Dalthinir asked Inga for an opportunity to speak with her. She agreed to meet with him the following day.

When they met, his resolve almost failed him. He had never seen her looking so beautiful. She'd done something with her hair, but it had more to do with her inner radiance. It didn't matter if he couldn't define it. The simple truth was that she took his breath away.

"Well?" she asked gently. "Was there something you wanted to say to me?" She seemed well aware of the effect she was having on him, and it didn't appear to displease her.

"Yes, there was...there is," he stammered. "It's...about my future." He took a deep breath to steady himself. "When we last spoke I told you the future seemed bleak for me."

Her expression was unreadable.

"It's finally clear to me what I need to do."

A wary look had come over her face.

"I feel responsible. I am the one who saw what Banadin had been up to. The way he and his band of followers have behaved since then makes it obvious they have a lot to hide. I could easily keep an eye on them, and I'd do it willingly. But Adrastas has banned me. He refuses to see them as any kind of threat. If the Compact won't act in its own defense and in defense of the kingdom, someone else has to. That's why it's my responsibility."

She was beginning to look alarmed. "What are you saying?"

"I need to leave the Compact."

"You can't do that!" Panic was twisting her lovely face, and it wrenched his heart.

"I don't have any choice."

"Leaving is a sentence of death!"

"I understand that. I'm willing to take my chances."

"I can't believe I'm hearing this! There must be some way I can talk you out of it. I know that Roza and Clarree and their friends have made your life unbearable. I've done nothing to support you, and I'm sorry about that. I truly am! But don't let them force you out! They're not worth it!"

"They're not the ones driving me away. I'll be glad to see the last of them, and I won't pretend otherwise. But it's Adrastas who's forced me to leave. He's prevented me from doing what I know I must do."

"Then I'm going to speak with him. And I'm going to do it right now! Promise me you won't do anything rash! Not before you've spoken to him."

He nodded reluctantly. "Very well."

She would almost certainly be wasting her breath. Adrastas wasn't known for backing down once he'd made a decision. But she didn't need anyone to tell her that.

She stormed off, like a hen in defense of her chicks. He watched her in hopeless admiration. A future with her would never be possible, even if both of them wanted it. Not if he followed through on what he needed to do.

Then it struck him. She'd backed away from him after he told her his future seemed bleak. Did she see that as a rejection? Could she have heard him to be suggesting a future with her would seem bleak to him? If so, she couldn't be more wrong. Leaving her would be the most difficult thing about leaving the Compact.

She was gone for several hours, but eventually she found him.

"Adrastas will see you first thing in the morning." she told him breathlessly. "He will come to you. Remember your promise!"

He nodded. "I can't pretend I'm optimistic. But thank you anyway, Inga."

She stared at him with a strange look on her face. It wouldn't have surprised him if she'd yelled at him. Or even if she'd told him he mattered to her. But she turned on her heel and left without saying anything.

The next morning Adrastas tracked him down as promised. He looked equal parts bemused, annoyed, and concerned. "What's going on, Dalthinir?" he asked, frowning.

"Do you see Masters Clarree, Roza, and Garmer as a threat?" Dalthinir asked.

"Look, I've heard they've been targeting you. I'm going to speak to them about it."

"I'm not talking about that."

"If you're asking whether I believe they're part of some hidden conspiracy to bring down the kingdom, then no, I don't."

"And you refuse to allow me to keep an eye on them with farsense?"

"I have no intention of lifting that ban, so don't bother asking."

Dalthinir nodded calmly. "Then I don't think there's anything for us to talk about."

Adrastas's brows drew together. "You're not seriously considering leaving the Compact?"

Dalthinir didn't answer.

"Let me make it absolutely clear to you. If you leave, you'll be declared a renegade. You know what that means. When someone refuses to come under the authority of the Compact, we are required by law to hunt them down and execute them. You do understand that, don't you?"

He inclined his head. He understood well enough. The policy had been implemented after a near disaster many years ago. The king at the time had told the mages they needed to deal with their own malcontents if they wanted to preserve the Compact's cherished independence from the Crown. In practice, it meant that being declared a renegade was a sentence of death.

"I don't want that to happen to you," Adrastas continued. "I'm appealing to you personally—don't even consider it!"

Dalthinir continued to hold his peace. He and Adrastas both knew that if they wanted to execute someone, they would need to catch them first.

Adrastas started to become irritated. "I have no interest in hunting other mages. It's a distraction I can't afford."

When there was still no response, he added in frustration, "You won't last a month if you become a renegade! How will that prevent your conspirators doing whatever it is you think they're going to do?"

Finally Dalthinir spoke. "Thank you for your visit."

Adrastas stared at him in perplexity. "I'll have strong words with the others and tell them to back off. The rest is up to you, Dalthinir."

He turned away, shaking his head.

Inga appeared the following day. "Adrastas told me what happened," she said. "Are you determined to go through with it?"

He nodded his head.

Tears came to her eyes. "I'm begging you, Dalthinir, don't do this!"

He could hardly bear to look at her. "It isn't because I want to leave you," he told her miserably.

"If that isn't what you want, then why are you even considering it?"

Too distressed to wait for an answer, she turned away and left him.

Shaken by her reaction, for the first time he began to question whether he could actually go through with it. With Inga at his side he knew he could bear whatever Roza and the others served up. As for everything else, the more he thought about it, the more he doubted himself. How substantial were the perils he feared? What if the threat truly had ended with Banadin? He had assumed Banadin was using his notaries to pass on dangerous plans to his followers through his will, but he knew nothing for certain. Maybe the will did no more than distribute assets, perhaps after delays to allow younger beneficiaries to come of age. Could he throw his life away based on an assumption?

That night he went to bed more confused and uncertain than at any time in his life.

When he eventually managed to get to sleep, he dreamed. There was a familiar feel to it, and even in his dream state he was able to recall his experience in the cavern—drifting upward with the moth before racing through the underground river behind the fish.

Now he was rising upward in the dark. The air was cold, but it didn't trouble him. Above him he saw the numberless stars stretched out in a dazzling display. Looking down, he glimpsed tiny winking lights below him—the city of Cambrick. The cliffs at the rear of the city were slipping away beneath him, and he saw that he was wheeling north. He traveled on, unaware of the passage of time. As before, he felt calm and detached.

Eventually the sun rose on his right hand. He saw that he was high above the ground, traveling swiftly. The rays of the sun picked out a series of peaks ahead. Beyond the mountains he caught a glimpse of sunlight reflecting on water, and he realized he had almost reached the sea.

He sensed rather than saw human figures below him, stepping into a hidden chamber in the mountains to open a forbidden book. Anger, fierce and terrible, pulsed through the atmosphere around him.

A bright flash blotted out the sun as an unimaginable eruption of magic was released. Great trees below him were flattened as if they were twigs.

For the first time he perceived that he was perched on the back of a dragon, golden in the sunlight. His steed withstood the force of the blast. Turning its back on the mountains, it flew back the way it had come.

Above him a lowering cloud of darkness veiled the sun. Below him he witnessed the aftermath of the shock wave. It had torn through the kingdom, destroying everything in its path.

Finally they reached the cliffs overlooking Cambrick. As the dragon landed at the top of the cliffs, he slipped off its back. Moving to the edge of the precipice, he gazed down at the broken remnants of a once thriving city. Nothing moved in the desolation. The capital and its inhabitants had ceased to exist.

. . .

DALTHINIR WOKE WITH A START, the dream still real in his mind. It had been much more than a dream. It was a portent, a warning.

He remembered the dream that precipitated his escape through the underground river. It, too, had offered a vision of what might be, if he dared to bring it to fruition. This time he was being shown what would happen if he failed to act.

Providence had surely played a part before. He had been guided to the sunlight, emerging with the conviction that he escaped because there were things he needed to do. He couldn't doubt that Providence was at work again.

It was impossible to ignore the fact that his life would soon have ended had he ignored the earlier dream. How could he ignore the latest one? He rose from his bed with an unshakable conviction that much more than his life would end if he failed to heed the warning. It was impossible to guess when the crisis might arise, but somehow he would know.

After going to sleep troubled and perplexed, he realized all his confusion and uncertainty had evaporated, like mist before the morning sun.

Leaving the Compact had become his key priority, and he quickly packed whatever basic supplies he could comfortably carry. Winding up his affairs would alert others. He could only leave things as they were.

One thing could not be left undone. Retrieving a quill and a small piece of parchment, he sat down to write.

 Inga,
   I know my decision will make no sense to you, but I am doing what I believe to be right, whatever the cost. Please know that I have no desire to hurt you. I will cherish the memory of you always.
   D

RISING WELL before dawn the following day, he hurried to Inga's quarters and slipped his parchment under her door. Then he made his way to the city gates, leaving as soon as they were opened.

He had left a second parchment inside his quarters, addressed to the chief master. It was brief and to the point.

> To Chief Master Adrastas,
>
> I am leaving the Compact with regret. Please know that I bear no ill will to anyone. You can be assured that I will never seek to harm the kingdom or its people.
> Dalthinir

He had considered carefully before writing that he bore no ill will to anyone. But it was true. Having seen the way hatred twisted people, he had decided he could not afford the luxury of hating. Bitterness and unforgiveness had a way of preventing people from acting in their own best interests. He would never condone the behavior of Banadin and his followers, and he would work tirelessly to frustrate their attempts to do harm. But he refused to waste energy despising them.

His immediate concern was to get as far from the city as possible before his absence was discovered. Adrastas had made it clear what would happen. He would be hunted down and killed.

Throwing his life away had never been his intention. It wouldn't be possible to prevent a disaster from the grave.

A long ride in the cart of a friendly farmer gave him a solid start. When they finally parted ways, he was far from the city.

For better or worse he had done it. There was no turning back now.

DALTHINIR LAY SHIVERING in the stream as its waters flowed around him.

The months since he left the Compact had included a number of close calls. From the beginning there had always been a party of mages pursuing him, and the hunters had been relentless. Banadin's followers had invariably been numbered among the pursuers. The hunters had always included Master Roza, who also boasted the rare ability to detect magical auras, and Master Clarree, who shared some of the other abilities of the fugitive, although with less power.

Never had they come so close to catching him. In his desperation he had been forced to immerse himself in a stream, knowing that water would mask his glimmer. But he wouldn't be able to bear the cold for much longer.

Protecting himself with a shield was a simple task for Dalthinir. He could shield himself from physical and magical attacks. If he could only shield his glimmer, Roza wouldn't be able to find him. He shook his head in frustration.

He recalled the dream that had finally driven him from the Compact. The dragon's anger had been palpable, as solid as the creature that bore him aloft, highlighting the significance of what he was witnessing. The dragon might have been a symbol, but Dalthinir had sensed there was nothing symbolic about the mission entrusted to him.

How could Providence expect him to prevent a disaster if he was captured and executed? It made no sense.

The cold of the water was becoming too much to endure. He could warm himself magically, but the mages hunting him were camped little more than a stone's throw away. Any use of his power would be easily detectable from there.

Recognizing that he could remain in the water no longer, he prepared himself for the inevitable.

As he moved toward the bank, a memory came unbidden to his mind—an image of the golden dragon hidden in the cliffs beside Cambrick. He had sensed it was richly sheathed in magic. That made no sense, since the creature surely could not have been real. He hadn't detected a magical aura, which was no surprise. Even if it had been real, dragons were reputedly able to mask their glimmer.

Absorbed in the full intensity of the creature's magic, he crawled out of the water onto the bank of the stream and surrounded himself with a shield. His magical aura would now be visible to Roza, and any other mage able to detect it. Even his use of power in creating a shield would be detectable this close to the other mages.

He was close enough to the hunters to faintly hear them speak, but as the minutes slipped by, there was no reaction of any kind, from Roza or anyone else. Astonished, Dalthinir turned his attention toward his shield. He saw at once that it included an unfamiliar component. Was it a new layer of shielding that masked his magical aura? Having recognized it, he was confident he could draw upon it again.

At that moment Lars, who was a member of the party on that occasion, stepped away from the group. On impulse, Dalthinir wrapped a shield around him consisting only of the new component. Lars would not be aware of the shield, so there would be no particular risk.

Very soon he heard Roza calling, "Where have you gone, Lars? Are you all right?"

He hastily removed the shield.

"Can't a man take a private moment to relieve himself?" replied Lars irritably.

"No matter! For some reason your glimmer vanished for a moment."

Dalthinir was astonished, but he wasted no time in slipping away from the party. Now that he could mask his glimmer, he was increasingly confident they would never find him.

In the days that followed, he discovered that he was also able to use a shield to mask his use of power. Such masking itself used power, effectively halving the amount of power available to him. But it seemed a small price to pay. Curiously, he was also able to confuse his magical footprint, so that even if he allowed his magical aura or his use of power to be detected, they were not recognizable as his own.

As well as shielding his own magical aura and his use of power, he was able to do the same for other mages. He could see little immediate benefit from it, but he stored the information away for later use.

With these two new capabilities at his disposal, he was never seriously at risk of capture again.

Dalthinir quickly developed a reputation for being invisible. The years passed, and he showed no hint of aggressive or malicious intent toward anyone. His sources were able to confirm that those mages who hadn't forgotten him gradually came to ignore him entirely.

EPILOGUE

Ten long years had passed since Dalthinir declared himself renegade and left the Compact. With his fellow mages blind to the possible dangers posed by Banadin and his followers, he had departed with a determination to remain constantly alert, poised to respond to any threat. In the early days he had worked hard to cultivate a number of sources that allowed him to stay abreast of events from a distance.

As if in mockery of his vigilance, there had been no obvious sign of dangerous schemes for him to thwart in the years that followed. Not surprisingly, he sometimes wondered if he had been a fool for leaving. He pictured still a dark-haired mage gazing up at him with concern in her eyes.

Apart from Inga, though, he had few regrets. He had led a rich and varied life. While always hiding his true identity, he had usually worked openly as a mage, helping out on farms and in small villages in remote areas where Compact mages never ventured. He had also aided fishermen, sailing far out to sea with them in their flimsy vessels. A warm welcome now awaited him in many parts of the kingdom.

When he knew the people he helped could afford it, he had accepted payment of various kinds for his labors. Caches of the coins he had received now lay hidden in a number of key locations against a day when he might need them.

Even though he was occasionally well compensated, he had invested a considerable proportion of his effort among people of few means. With his survival dependent on remaining hidden, much of his time had been spent in isolated locations. That had allowed him to witness first hand the lot of the poor and disadvantaged. The experience had been confronting, and he had done whatever he could to ease their suffering. His previous life now seemed impossibly out of touch with reality.

Curiously, although none of his three main persecutors—Masters Clarree, Roza, and Garmer—had been old when he left, each of them had died in the years that followed. He had played no part in their demise, and their deaths had reportedly resulted from natural causes.

He had often wondered what brought about the death of Banadin, and the subsequent passing of the mage's three most powerful disciples had raised the issue anew. Had they fallen victim to their own research? It was impossible to know. However it had happened, the passage of time had achieved what the Compact failed to do, delivering justice impartially.

Masters Petria and Lars remained. If they had plans to continue where Banadin left off, they'd shown no sign of it.

However he had no reason to assume that attentiveness was no longer necessary. He had not forgotten what he learned from the maid. Banadin's will included instructions for the future distribution of unspecified items. The situation could change in a moment when that happened. It wouldn't surprise him at all if Banadin had intentionally waited long enough for everyone to become comfortable and relaxed.

With that in mind, a time had come when he began to wonder if he had allowed his new priorities to dull his watchfulness. Closely monitoring Banadin's remaining acolytes had never been practical from a distance. It was unthinkable that he might undo years of alertness by responding too late when a crisis finally arose.

He saw only one way forward. Setting aside the risk, he had relocated to the capital a couple of years previously. With almost every mage in the kingdom in close proximity, his ability to hide his magical aura became more crucial than ever. Even so he could never afford to relax. He couldn't know when someone might spot him and recognize him.

Once in the capital it became easier to monitor Lars and Petria directly. For two years he watched and waited, observing no patterns of behavior that might hint at a change.

Then came a day when, wandering the streets with his hood pulled low over his face as usual, he noticed that a crowd had formed. Sensing a small but steady outpouring of power, he edged closer to investigate.

A sudden flare of magic startled him, and not just because of its strength. Familiar as he was with the unique power footprint of every mage in the city, this was a burst of power he didn't recognize. It surprised him even more when he identified the source.

An injustice was about to be done, and seeing it, he acted without hesitation. For someone who had long refused to turn away from the suffering of others, it was an easy decision.

Never could he have imagined what would follow.

After lying hidden and forgotten for many years, he was about to be exposed to the baying hounds once more. Only time would tell if life as a renegade had equipped him for all that was to come.

The End

Dalthinir's story continues in
The Hard Edge of Magic
(The Ruptured Kingdom Book 1)
by Allan N. Packer

NOTE FROM THE AUTHOR

Thank you for reading *The Renegade: A Prequel to The Hard Edge of Magic* —I hope you enjoyed it. Thank you, too, for joining my mailing list at www.allanpacker.com. If you'd like to reach out to me for any reason, I'd love to hear from you!

If you've already read *The Hard Edge of Magic (The Ruptured Kingdom Book 1)*, I hope the novelette provided useful background to Dalthinir and the journey that led him to become a renegade. It should also provide additional background to the world described in *The Hard Edge of Magic*.

If this novelette is your introduction to *The Ruptured Kingdom* series, you can discover more about Dalthinir in *The Hard Edge of Magic* and subsequent novels.

Note that paperback and audiobook editions of *The Renegade: A Prequel to The Hard Edge of Magic* are available through online retailers.

In case you are not already aware of my first epic fantasy series, *The Stone Cycle* saga begins with *The Stone of Knowing (Book 1)* and *The Cost of Knowing (Book 2)*. The two books together form a complete story (they are not standalone novels, and should be read in order). The saga continues with *The Stone of Authority (Book 3)*, *The Struggle for Authority*

(Book 4), *The Stone of Vitality (Book 5)*, and concludes with *The Hope of Vitality (Book 6)*.

As a subscriber to my mailing list at my website (*www.allanpack er.com*), you can also download a second exclusive bonus novelette—a prequel to *The Cost of Knowing*, the second novel in *The Stone Cycle* series. The novelette, *The Rending*, is a complete story four chapters (13,000 words) in length that can be read independently of the novels in the series. It provides background information to a key character in the ongoing story, as well as revealing the origin of the community she leads. The novelette is described below.

Endings may be beginnings in disguise

Anneka is comfortable and confident, a noblewoman of consequence living a life of privilege. Until the day her world is torn apart.

After losing everything she most cares about, she must abandon her home and her way of life in an attempt to secure the future of those who depend on her.

No one, least of all Anneka, could anticipate a deeper significance to her struggle. Yet her journey will one day influence the fate of kingdoms.

ACKNOWLEDGMENTS

Special thanks to my beta readers, Merilyn, Adrian Herber, and Roly Edwardes. They offered excellent feedback and suggestions that improved the story. Big thanks too to my beta listener, Arpenny Hart, for her feedback on the audiobook version.

Kudos to 100 Covers, who promptly came up with a great cover.

My grateful thanks go to Brian Plush for the awesome map.

Finally, thanks go to God, who freely offers grace and forgiveness to renegades and hidebound legalists alike.

ABOUT THE AUTHOR

Allan Packer writes epic fantasy. *The Ruptured Kingdom* is his second series, following *The Stone of Knowing* and the later stories in *The Stone Cycle* series.

Allan grew up surrounded by books and became an avid reader during his childhood. In his university years fantasy displaced science fiction as his favorite genre, thanks primarily to J. R. R. Tolkien. He later shared this love with his four children by reading *The Lord of the Rings* to them aloud—a three-month marathon he completed twice during their formative years.

Born in Australia, Allan has lived and worked on three continents, and spent one quarter of his working years abroad. Having worked as an IT professional throughout his career, he was first published as a technical author.

Today he lives with his wife in Adelaide, South Australia, near their children and a growing band of grandchildren.

Allan is currently working on the latest installment in his series *The Ruptured Kingdom*.